The Happy-Hoppy Frog

Becky Freeman

Illustrated by

Matt Archambault

A Faith Parenting Guide can be found on page 32.

Faith Kids™ is an imprint of
Cook Communications Ministries, Colorado Springs, Colorado 80918
Cook Communications, Paris, Ontario
Kingsway Communications, Eastbourne, England

THE HAPPY-HOPPY FROG
© 2000 by Becky Freeman for text and Matthew Archambault for illustrations.

Published in association with the literary agency of Alive Communications, Inc., 1465 Kelly
Johnson Blvd., Suite 320, Colorado Springs, CO 80920.

Edited by Jeannie Harmon
Designed by Ya Ye Design

Scripture taken from the *Holy Bible: New International Version®.* copyright © 1973, 1978, 1984 by
International Bible Society. Used by permission of Zondervan Publishing House. All rights
reserved.

First printing, 2000
Printed in Singapore
04 03 02 01 00   5 4 3 2 1

Library of Congress Cataloging-in-Publication Data

Freeman, Becky, 1959-
    The happy hoppy frog/Becky Freeman: illustrated by Matt Archambault.
        p. cm. — (Gabe & critters)
    Summary: Gabe plans to enter Happy Hoppy, his pet frog, in a contest at the county fair, but
when his frog disappears, Gabe prays for God's help in finding him. Includes questions and
answers about frogs.
    ISBN 0-7814-3342-8
    [1. Frogs Fiction. 2. Fairs Fiction. 3. Christian life Fiction.]
I. Archambault, Matthew, ill. II. Title. III. Series: Freeman, Becky, 1959- Gabe & critters.
PZ7.F874636Hap 2000
[E]—dc21

                                                                                                99-41923
                                                                                                     CIP

Dedicated to:
My youngest son, Gabe,
a true critter-lover and
the inspiration for this series.
Thanks for the "worm" memories
. . . and for the hugs.
Love,
Mom

"Where are you going?" shouted Gabe as he watched his brothers, Zach and Zeke, load up the truck with sweet-smelling hay.

"We're taking Pete and Re-Pete to the County Fair!" said Zach.

"Do you think they'll win the Sloppiest Pig Contest?" Gabe asked.

Zeke tipped his cowboy hat at Gabe and teased, "Naw, Gabe. I think you'll win that prize!"

Gabe playfully socked his brother on the arm, then Zeke wrestled him to the ground. Mostly they just laughed and pretended to be fighting, but "roughhousin'" always made Mom nervous. Within seconds, she appeared at the front door, wiping her hands on a rag.

"You boys better knock it off before one of you gets hurt!"

The boys rose from the ground, brushing the dirt from their jeans.

Zeke looked at Mom and grinned. "Aw, Mom. I was just playin' with the little guy."

"Yeah, Mom," echoed Gabe, "he was just playing with the little guy."

"Never mind, you two, " said Mom. "Now, come help me carry these peach preserves out to the truck. Didn't your sister do a beautiful job?"

Rachel had been picking, peeling, slicing, boiling, sugaring, and canning peaches for days now. She was determined to win a ribbon at the county fair for her homemade preserves.

Just then, Dad's face appeared over the top of the shed roof. With eyes wide, Gabe watched his father walk around in front of the shed. Dad was ten feet tall, dressed in a red and white striped Uncle Sam suit. Gabe's mouth dropped open.

"Dad!" yelled Gabe. "You grew into a giant! What have you been eating?"

"It's not what I've been eating, Son. It's what I'm walking on. What do you think about these stilts?" Gabe loved having a dad who could do tricks like walking on stilts.

It looked like everyone in the family was doing something special for the fair: Dad would be the world's tallest announcer, Mom had sewn a special quilt, Rachel canned peaches, and Zach and Zeke were showing off Pete and Re-Pete. Everyone was doing something special except Gabe. What could he do at the fair?

Just then Happy-Hoppy, Gabe's pet frog, hopped out of a pocket and onto Gabe's shoulder. This gave Gabe a GREAT idea.

"Come on, Happy," Gabe said aloud as he tucked the frog back into his pocket. "We're going to enter a contest!"

As soon as the family truck pulled up at the fairgrounds, everyone scattered in different directions. Zach and Zeke carried Pete and Re-Pete to the Livestock Barn. Rachel and Mom headed toward the Home Living Show.

Dad looked way, way, way down at Gabe and said, "Son, you can go anywhere you want as long as you can see my legs. If you see my legs, I can see you. Just look up and holler if you need me!"

Then Dad began walking around shouting, "Welcome, one and all, to the Cotton County Fair!"

Gabe couldn't believe all the wonderful things going on—the food, the rides, the games! Where to begin? Then he saw the sign he'd been hoping to see. It read: Frog Jumpin' Contest. Starts at noon.

Gabe reached down to pat his pocket. It was flat! Where was Happy-Hoppy?

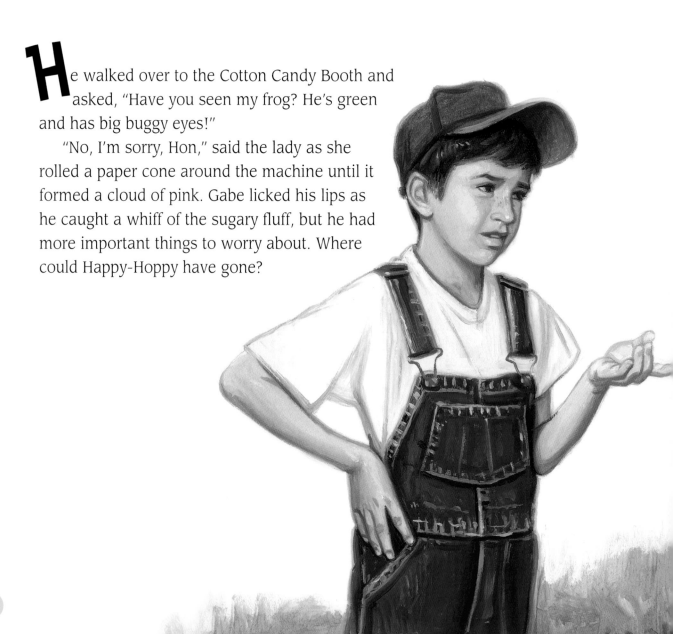

He walked over to the Cotton Candy Booth and asked, "Have you seen my frog? He's green and has big buggy eyes!"

"No, I'm sorry, Hon," said the lady as she rolled a paper cone around the machine until it formed a cloud of pink. Gabe licked his lips as he caught a whiff of the sugary fluff, but he had more important things to worry about. Where could Happy-Hoppy have gone?

Next Gabe wandered over to the Ferris wheel. Still, no Happy-Hoppy.

He called up to his dad. "Hey, up there!"

"What can I help you with, Gabe?"

"Can you see Happy-Hoppy?"

Dad looked all around the fairgrounds. No sign of the little green frog.

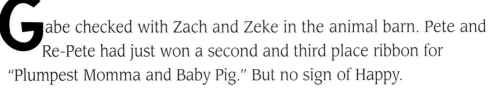

Gabe checked with Zach and Zeke in the animal barn. Pete and Re-Pete had just won a second and third place ribbon for "Plumpest Momma and Baby Pig." But no sign of Happy.

Mom and Rachel were hugging each other when Gabe ran up to the Home Living Booth. Rachel had won a first place ribbon for her "Prize Peach Preserves" and Mom had won a drawing for a shopping trip. But they had not seen Happy.

No one had seen Happy.

Gabe sat down and wondered what to do. Then he remembered what Dad had told him last night on the dock as they sat watching the stars.

"Son, if you're ever lost, say a prayer and look up," he'd said, "because, let me tell you something, God never loses you!"

So Gabe began to pray, "Dear God, please help me find my frog." As soon as he said, "Amen," he looked up, and there was Happy-Hoppy sitting on the brim of his hat.

Gabe took Happy and ran as fast as he could. It was almost noon and the contest would begin soon.

Mom, Zach, Zeke, Rachel, even Pete and Re-Pete gathered around to cheer for Gabe and his frog. Dad made the announcement for the jump to begin.

"Attention all frog-legged critters. On your mark. Get set. JUMP!"

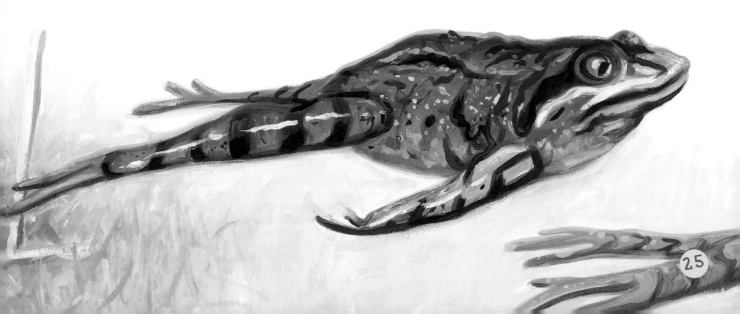

All the frogs made big jumps, but Happy had been practicing his hopping all day. He jumped so high, he jumped over the other frogs, over the winner's wall, and landed—SPLAT—on top of the judge's head.

"I believe we have a winner!" the judge shouted as he placed matching blue ribbons around Gabe and his pet frog. Everyone laughed with joy, but Gabe laughed the hardest of all.

Gabe's Fun Frog Facts

1. Frogs are animals we call amphibians. What is an amphibian?

Amphibians are animals that live two lives—most live in the water when they are young, then grow up to live on land. They are born with gills for breathing in water (just like fish), then they get lungs when they are grown.

2. What does it mean when they say that frogs are cold-blooded?

This means that frogs' insides are the same temperature as it is outside. Humans and mammals—like you and Gabe, stay warm inside no matter how hot or cold the temperature is outside. That's why toads and frogs often go underground in the winter (this is called *hibernating*). Otherwise, they'd freeze into amphibian popsicles! Even underground, frogs and toads are too cold to move, so they lie very still.

3. What do you call a baby frog?

A baby frog is called a *tadpole*. Tadpoles have no legs, but they have long tails. If you said they are called *polliwogs* you are also correct.

4. Where does the tadpole's tail go when it becomes a frog?

When a tadpole changes into a frog, it looks like its tail gets smaller. But it isn't really shrinking. It is turning into something else—a backbone, hind legs, and front legs.

5. What's the difference between a toad and a frog?

A toad is usually chubby with rough bumpy skin and no teeth. A frog is thinner, with smooth, moist skin and usually has teeth. Frogs also spend more of their adult lives in and near the water.

6. Can you get warts from a toad?

No, you cannot get warts from a toad. Somebody just made this story up and it got passed around. The rumor probably started because the toad looks like it is covered with warts.

7. How does a toad defend itself?

A toad squirts out a nasty tasting liquid from the bumps on its skin. This may keep an animal from eating it. If you catch a toad and it lets out some of this liquid, be careful not to rub your eyes! The liquid will make them sore.

8. What do frogs eat?

Frogs eat mosquitoes, flies, moths, beetles, small crayfish, and worms. Their mouths are large and their long sticky tongues are attached to the front of their mouths, not the back. This way a frog's tongue can quickly flip out to catch insects for lunch. Yum, yum!

9. How far can a frog really jump?

The longest frog jump on record is seventeen feet and four inches.
Can you measure off seventeen feet and see how long that is?

10. What is the world's largest frog?

The world's largest frog is the Goliath frog of West Africa. The biggest one ever caught weighed more than seven pounds and was almost a yard long with its legs spread out. How do you think Gabe would like a frog that big?

Critter Project

Frog Drawing

Here's an easy way to draw a frog. See if you can do it!

1. Draw an oval for the face and two circles for the eyes. Draw in the mouth and eyes as above.

2. Draw two back legs and feet as shown above.

3. Draw two front feet.

Try your own drawing here!

God's Word Says

Trust the Lord with all your heart. Don't depend on your own understanding. Remember the Lord in everything you do. And he will give you success.

Proverbs 3:5,6 (NIV)

The Happy-Hoppy Frog

Age: 4-7 years old

Life Issue: My child needs to understand that God is always watching over him or her, and will provide help when it is needed.

Spiritual Building Block: Trust

Learning Styles

Sight: Watch a video that shows Jesus performing miracles. How was Jesus able to help people? Can He help us today? Look up Luke 11:9, 10 in your Bible and explain its meaning to your child. Help your child to memorize as much as is appropriate for his or her age.

Sound: The next time you hear an emergency vehicle's siren, talk to your child about what the siren means. Is the vehicle going to help someone? How do we know? We can trust that an ambulance or fire truck is rushing to help someone in need because we have seen it happen before. How can we trust God to help us when we are in need?

Touch: Gather family members together and blindfold one person in the group. Turn that person around several times and have other family members direct him or her to walk through the house without bumping into furniture or walls. Talk about the importance of trusting your guide. How is God like the person giving you directions? Can we trust God to lead us in the right direction?